GUIDED MEMORIES

*Recording Your Personal Autobiography
On Video Or Audio Cassette*

Led By

David E. Zuccolotto

R & Z
Publishing Company, Inc.

ISBN 0-9634378-0-1

Printed in the United States Of America.

Cover design by Joal Morris.
Graphic illustrations by Micorgrafx.

Guided Memories
Record of Completion

_____
Name

_____
_____
_____
Address

_____
Age

_____
Date of Birth

_____
Place of Birth

_____
Date You Began Guided Memories

_____
Date You Finished Guided Memories

To my mother
who taught me the importance
of values, traditions and memories

INTRODUCTION

Generations come and generations go,

but the earth remains forever....

There is no remembrance of people of old,

and even those who are yet to come

will not be remembered by those who follow.

Ecclesiastes

ou are unlike anyone before you, or anyone yet to live. You have traveled certain paths in life that could only come from YOUR choices, values and opinions. These travels form a creative map of your personality and spirit as a human being; a map future generations can use as an invaluable guide for their own journey.

Values, traditions and memories serve an essential role in the harmony and strength of a family. Children need to know they can explore and conquer the journey of life just as their relatives before them. They need to know that, although we are each unique as human beings, we all share in the search for meaning, pleasure, understanding and purpose.

Research has shown that families rich in the traditions and memories of their past are more likely to have the unity and strength necessary to meet the future. Unfortunately, a generation comes and goes, without parents leaving their children the valuable memories of their heritage.

This is especially important for those who have already traveled much of life's journey. As parents and grandparents grow older there is an increasing awareness of the need to give the next generation a world of hope and promise. There is the desire to educate a younger generation, providing them with the insight and understanding to appreciate the lives of others, as well as themselves; and nothing is more powerful than the unique experience of your life!

How, then, does one record their memories? What should be included? How should it be organized? These questions make recording one's memories seem overwhelming. However, with the Guided Memories Workbook recording your autobiography is easy and fun. Guided Memories will help you organize the cherished memories of your life into a simple, neatly designed program to be recorded on video or audio cassette. It is a fulfilling and enjoyable way of passing on your memories to be appreciated and enjoyed by those you love. It is an investment you will be proud of and a treasure future generations will cherish forever.

David Zuccolotto
Family Therapist

The growth of the human mind is still high adventure,
In many ways the highest adventure on earth.
And nothing is more characteristic of that growth
Than the transmission of vital thought and experience
From one person to another and from one generation to Another.

Normon Cousins

INSTRUCTIONS

The Guided Memories Workbook is a way for you to record those memories of life which best reflect your unique personality and record them on audio or video cassette. The outline below provides an overview of the workbook and how it is organized. You will find the instructions easy to follow, making Guided Memories an enjoyable and worthwhile adventure.

The workbook is divided into four sections:

I. PICTURES TO REMEMBER

II. TIME FLIES

III. PERSONALITY & OPINIONS

IV. LESSONS TO REMEMBER

Each section leads you through simple steps to record your memories. However, there are similarities that all four sections share in common and are outlined below: Browse through the entire workbook and become familiar with its contents.

Worksheets are provided to ask you questions and help organize your thoughts for each section. The worksheets, along with the CUE CARDS, will be the information from which you record your memories on to video or audio cassette.

CUE CARDS

Cue cards are an aid for the actual recording of your memories. They include questions and/or statements that you read out loud (while being recorded), followed by your answer. They are intended to guide you in this process and serve as your "script." However, you may decide to reword or even eliminate certain cues. **You** are the director of your Guided Memories autobiography and are in charge of what to include or exclude from your final production.

VIDEO STEPS & IDEAS

Before beginning the exercises in the workbook decide if you will be recording with Video or Audio cassettes. If you will be using a video camera to record your memories follow the directions under this symbol . The workbook is designed for video or audio recording; **you** choose which recording method is most comfortable and easiest for you. Although the workbook will provide "Steps and Ideas" for you to follow, it is only a guide. **You** decide if you want to have someone record you or use a tripod and do it yourself. Be creative, choosing different locations for shooting--outdoors, different rooms in your house, etc. The workbook is your "script" and you are the director!

It is recommended that you use a high quality tape for recording. You may want to use four different videos for each of the four sections in the workbook and label each video with the title of that section. For example, your first video would be labeled, *"PART I - Pictures To Remember."* However, you can use the same tape to record more than one section and label your video accordingly. **MOST IMPORTANTLY, TAKE YOUR TIME!!!!!!**

AUDIO STEPS & IDEAS

If you will be using audio cassettes to record your memories follow the directions under this symbol . As mentioned above, the workbook is designed for video or audio recording; you choose which recording method is most comfortable and easiest for you. Be creative, adding music to the background of your recording, or have people ask you questions from the Guided Memories exercises. Remember, you are the director!

Be sure to use a high quality tape for recording. It is best to use different cassettes for each of the four sections in the workbook and label each cassette with the title of that section. For example, your first cassette would be labeled, *"PART I - Pictures To Remember."* If you use more than one cassette per section, label the additional cassettes, *"PART IA--Pictures To Remember,"* etc. However, you can use the same tape to record more than one section and label your cassette accordingly. **MOST IMPORTANTLY, TAKE YOUR TIME!!!!!!**

When Guided Memories has been completed you will have a collection of either video or audio cassettes, in addition to the material in the workbook. If you wish, you may fill out the order form on page 91, to purchase a Video or Audio Cassette Album to fit the type of tapes you have used. The album is covered with attractive art work and is a wonderful way to preserve your tapes and present as a gift to those you love.

When future generations listen to your Guided Memories Album they will have both the tapes and your workbook. This will help them appreciate the instructions you followed and what was involved in the production of your recordings. It will help the listener (and YOU!) understand that Guided Memories is not intended to capture all your life; nor is it intended to be a professional recording to impress your friends and family with your acting, speaking or editing ability. Rather, Guided Memories should reflect your sincere and natural way of communicating, capturing the "down to earth" and spontaneous character that makes you, uniquely YOU!

VIDEO & AUDIO CASSETTE ALBUMS

Let us examine our own lives and the lives of others.
Let us try to remember our own lives and examine the remembrance
of other lives in autobiographies, and let us see what
it would be to see with the eyes of the child, the youth, the man,
and the older man.

John Dune

PART I

Pictures To Remember

In primitive tribes we observe that the old people are almost always the guardians of the mysteries and the laws, and it is in these that the cultural heritage of the tribe is expressed. How does the matter stand with us? Where is the wisdom of our old people, where are the precious secrets and their visions?

C.J. Jung

O n page 11 begins the *Pictures To Remember* photo album. Choose 20 personal photographs and attach one on each page where it says "Attach Photo Here," <u>and complete the worksheet opposite each page.</u> If possible, choose photos of **family members or relatives for all 20 pictures**. If you wish, you may include pictures of friends or other individuals who have "been like family" to you, however other sections will probably cover non-family members sufficiently. Finish this project before you proceed to the next step.

 VIDEO STEPS & IDEAS

1. Prepare all video equipment for filming and load with a high quality video.

2. Determine your location for filming and who will operate the camera. It is easiest if someone operates the camera for you, however you can use a tripod and simply walk into the picture while it is recording and begin talking. If you film yourself it is best to use something to sit on, which can be used to focus the camera to ensure that your picture is clear and that your body is centered in the frame. When finished filming, walk out of the picture frame and turn the camera off.

3. When ready to film turn on the recorder and use the worksheets and cue cards as your script. Begin with your first photo and talk about the picture you have placed in the workbook. Talk freely, referring to the worksheet and cue cards until you have included all you would like to mention (however, remember you can't cover everything!). For example, you might say something like, *"The photo on page 13 is a picture of a family picnic and the one I want to tell you about is my father...oh, I forgot to tell you something else, he was 20 years old in this picture and, uhm...well, let me look at my cue cards for a minute....oh yeah, let me tell you about....."* When you have completed all twenty photos label your video with the title, *Pictures To Remember* and store in a safe place.

4. Tips: • Use page 7 as a **Title Page** by filming it first before you begin recording your script. • Keep the camera rolling with as few breaks as possible • **<u>Don't edit anything!</u>** include the bloopers, shots of the sky, laughter, tears, mistakes, shifts of thought, a change of answer etc. Part of the joy for the future viewer is seeing it all.

AUDIO STEPS & IDEAS

1. Prepare your audio equipment for recording. Choose a quiet setting where your voice can be heard clearly and you won't be bothered with interruptions, phone calls, door bells, etc.

2. When ready to record turn on the recorder and use the worksheets and cue cards as your script. Begin with your first photo and talk about the picture you have placed in the workbook. Talk freely, referring to the worksheet and cue cards until you have said all you would like to mention (however, remember you can't cover everything!) For example, you might say something like, *"The photo on page 13 is a picture of a family picnic and the one I want to tell you about is my father...oh, I forgot to tell you something else he was 20 years old in this picture and, uhm...well, let me look at my cue cards for a minute....oh yeah, let me tell you about....."* When you have completed all twenty photos label your cassette with the title, ***Pictures To Remember*** and store in a safe place.

3. **Tips:** • Before you begin talking about each photo, record what you will be discussing. For example, you might say something like, " I am going to be talking about the 20 pictures I want to be remembered." • Keep the recorder rolling with as few breaks as possible • **Don't edit anything!** include the bloopers, laughter, tears, mistakes, shifts of thought, a change of answer, etc. Part of the joy for future listeners is hearing it all.

Pictures To Remember

 **WORKSHEET**

Who is in this picture and who will I be talking about?

Approximately when was this picture taken?

Notes:

 CUE CARDS

(Note: If the person is still living, refer to in the present tense. Use the cue cards freely, paraphrasing, changing and creating your own. Or you can just read them and answer.)

" The name of the person I want to tell you about..."

" The picture was taken in the year......"

" One of the things we shared in common, that made us close was...."

" One of the things that made us different was...."

" What I would like my family (or close friends) to remember about him/her is....."

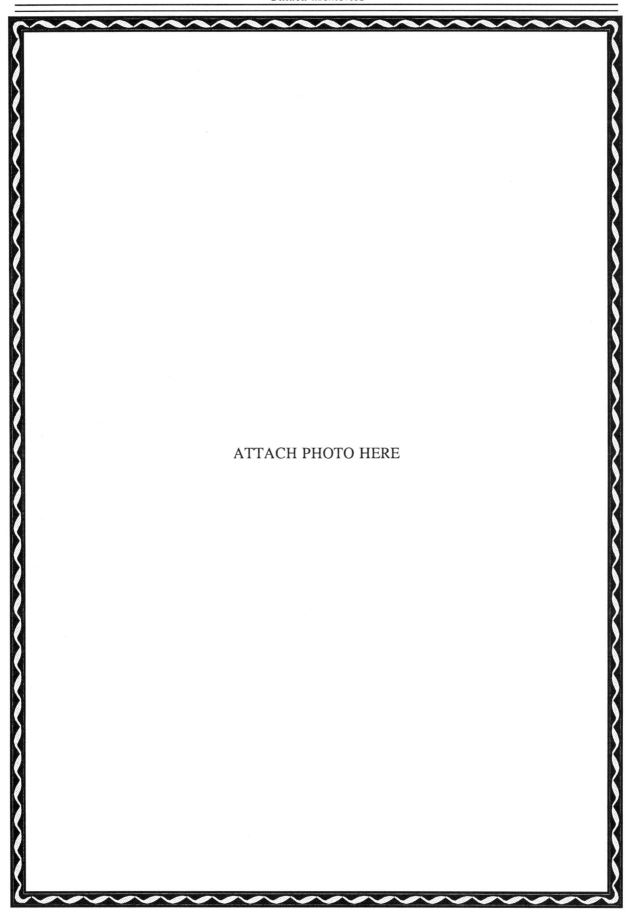

ATTACH PHOTO HERE

WORKSHEET

Who is in this picture and who will I be talking about?

Approximately when was this picture taken?

Notes:

CUE CARDS

(Note: If the person is still living, refer to him or her in the present tense.)

" The name of the person I want to tell you about...."

" The picture was taken in the year......"

" One of the things we shared in common, that made us close was...."

" One of the things that made us different was...."

" What I would like my family (or close friends) to remember about him/her is....."

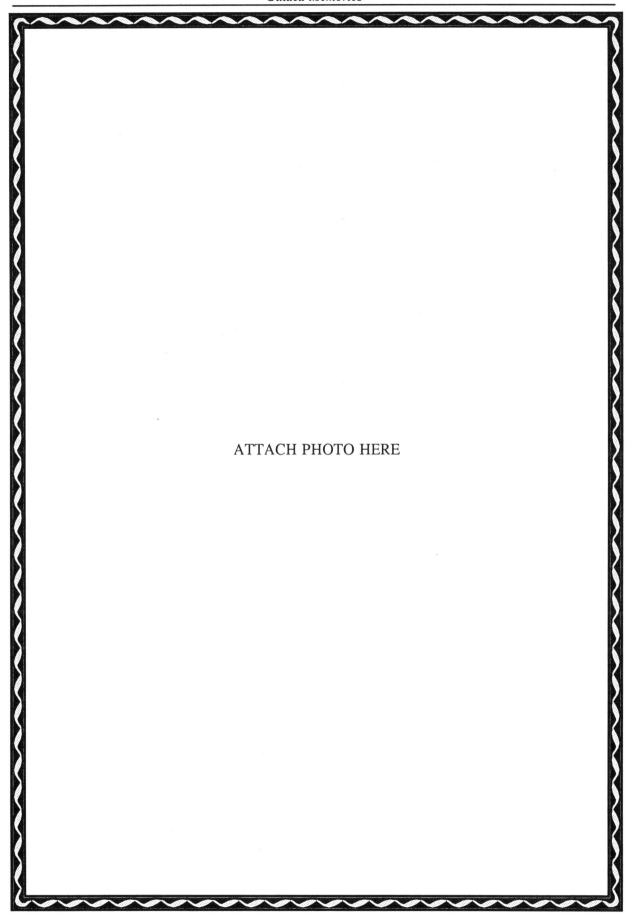

ATTACH PHOTO HERE

WORKSHEET

Who is in this picture and who will I be talking about?

Approximately when was this picture taken?

Notes:

CUE CARDS

(Note: If the person is still living, refer to him or her in the present tense.)

" The name of the person I want to tell you about...."

" The picture was taken in the year......"

" One of the things we shared in common, that made us close was...."

" One of the things that made us different was...."

" What I would like my family (or close friends) to remember about him/her is....."

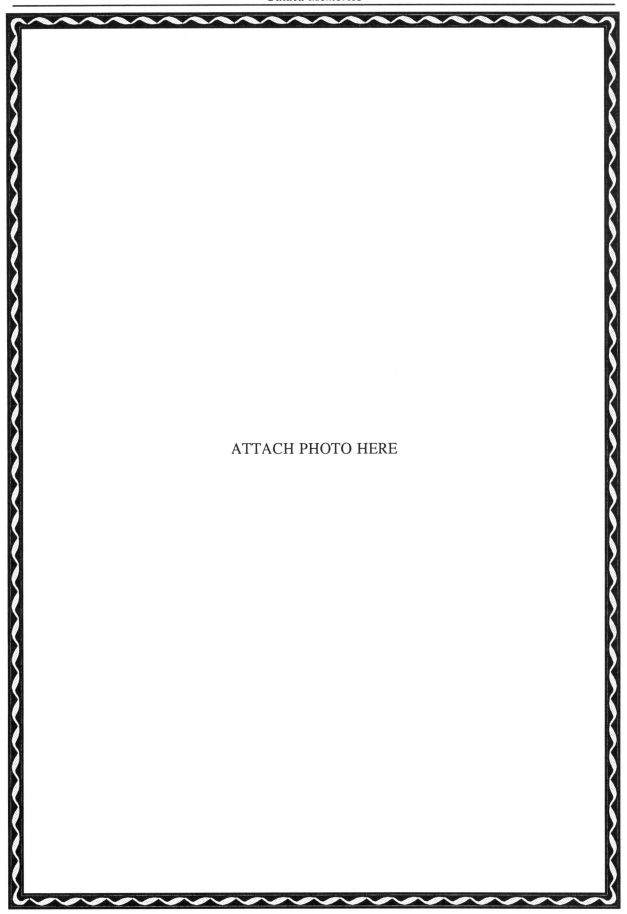

ATTACH PHOTO HERE

 **WORKSHEET**

Who is in this picture and who will I be talking about?

Approximately when was this picture taken?

Notes:

 CUE CARDS

(Note: If the person is still living, refer to him or her in the present tense.)

" The name of the person I want to tell you about ..."

" The picture was taken in the year......"

" One of the things we shared in common, that made us close was...."

" One of the things that made us different was...."

" What I would like my family (or close friends) to remember about him/her is....."

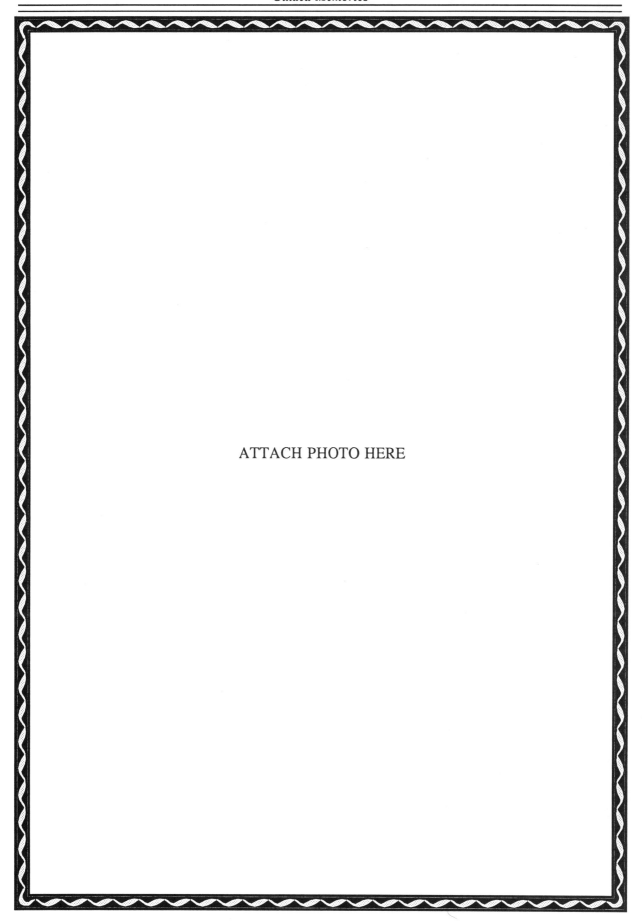

ATTACH PHOTO HERE

 **WORKSHEET**

Who is in this picture and who will I be talking about?

Approximately when was this picture taken?

Notes:

 CUE CARDS

(Note: If the person is still living, refer to him or her in the present tense.)

" The name of the person I want to tell you about..."

" The picture was taken in the year......"

" One of the things we shared in common, that made us close was...."

" One of the things that made us different was...."

" What I would like my family (or close friends) to remember about him/her is....."

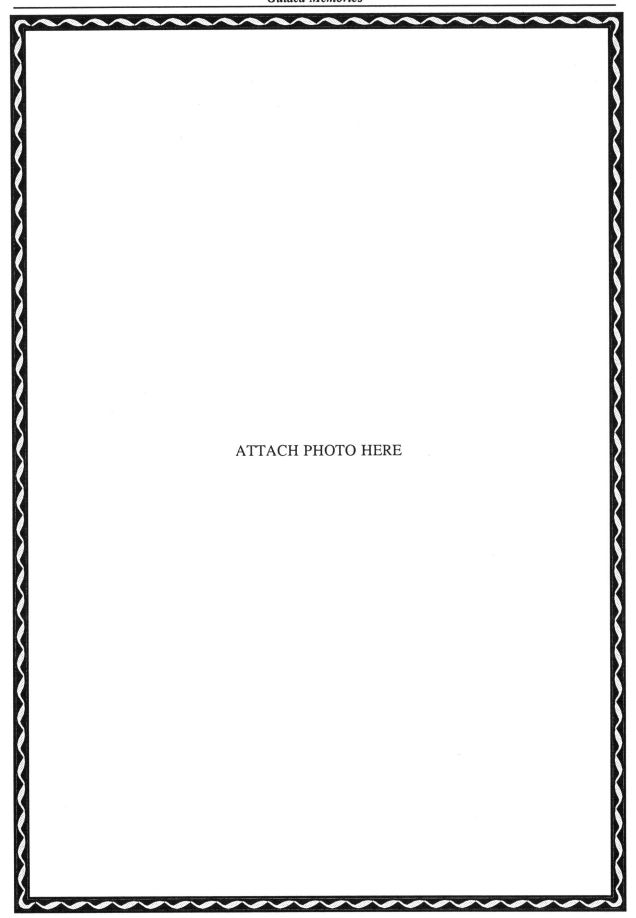

ATTACH PHOTO HERE

WORKSHEET

Who is in this picture and who will I be talking about?

Approximately when was this picture taken?

Notes:

CUE CARDS

(Note: If the person is still living, refer to him or her in the present tense.)

" The name of the person I want to tell you about...."

" The picture was taken in the year......"

" One of the things we shared in common, that made us close was...."

" One of the things that made us different was...."

" What I would like my family (or close friends) to remember about him/her is....."

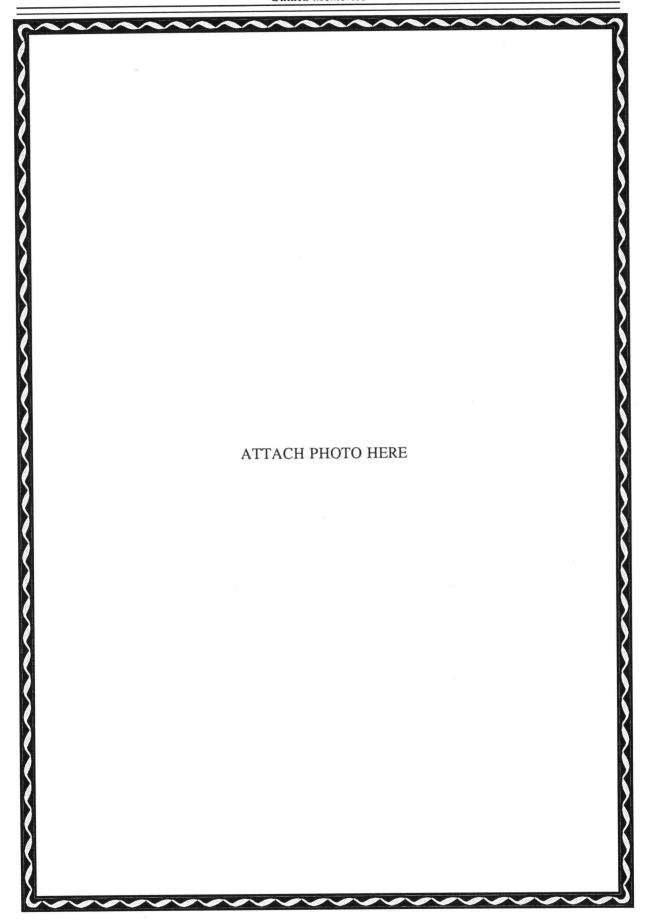

ATTACH PHOTO HERE

WORKSHEET

Who is in this picture and who will I be talking about?

Approximately when was this picture taken?

Notes:

CUE CARDS

(Note: If the person is still living, refer to him or her in the present tense.)

" The name of the person I want to tell you about...."

" The picture was taken in the year......"

" One of the things we shared in common, that made us close was...."

" One of the things that made us different was...."

" What I would like my family (or close friends) to remember about him/her is....."

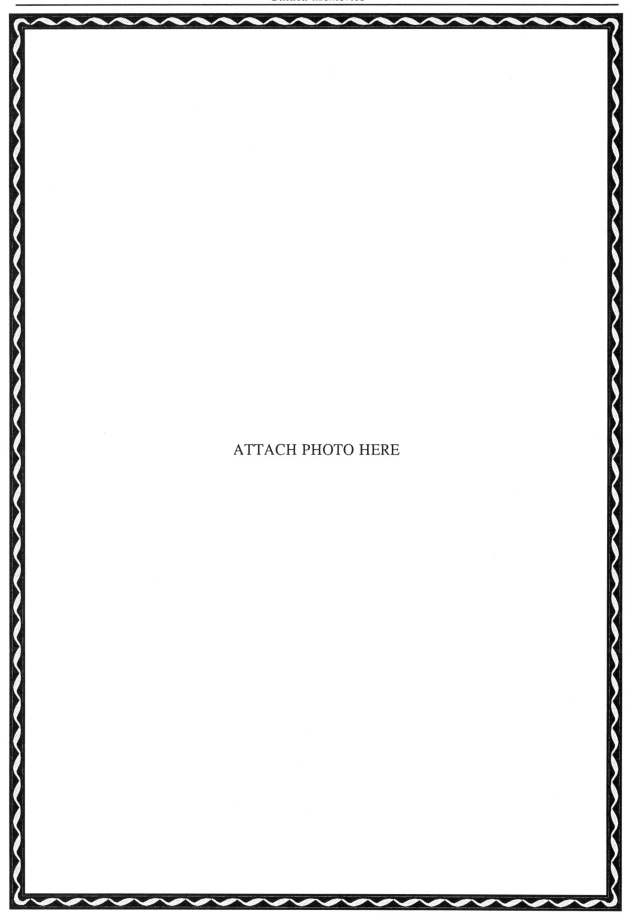

ATTACH PHOTO HERE

WORKSHEET

Who is in this picture and who will I be talking about?

Approximately when was this picture taken?

Notes:

CUE CARDS

(Note: If the person is still living, refer to him or her in the present tense.)

" The name of the person I want to tell you about...."

" The picture was taken in the year......"

" One of the things we shared in common, that made us close was...."

" One of the things that made us different was...."

" What I would like my family (or close friends) to remember about him/her is....."

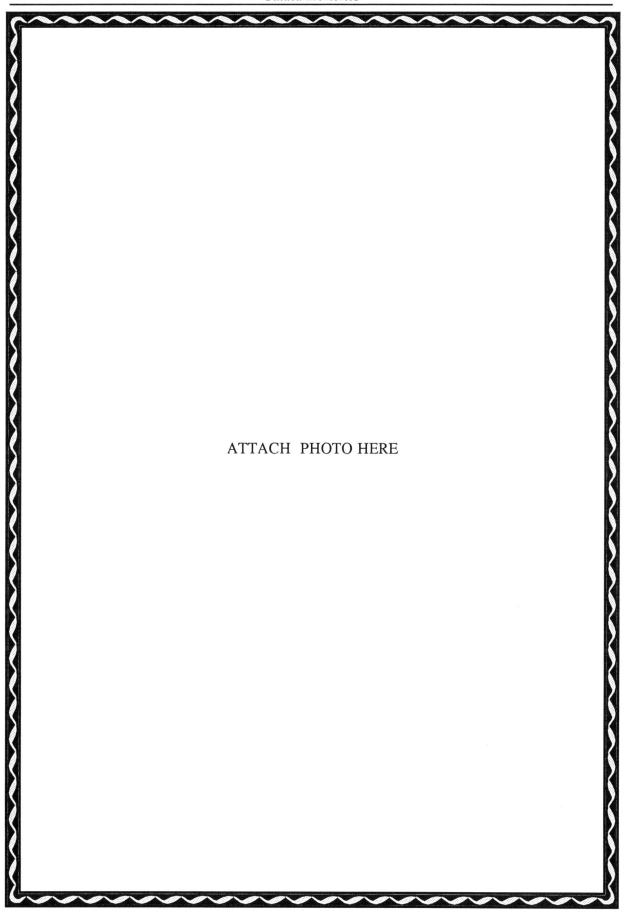

ATTACH PHOTO HERE

WORKSHEET

Who is in this picture and who will I be talking about?

Approximately when was this picture taken?

Notes:

CUE CARDS

(Note: If the person is still living, refer to him or her in the present tense.)

" The name of the person I want to tell you about...."

" The picture was taken in the year......"

" One of the things we shared in common, that made us close was...."

" One of the things that made us different was...."

" What I would like my family (or close friends) to remember about him/her is....."

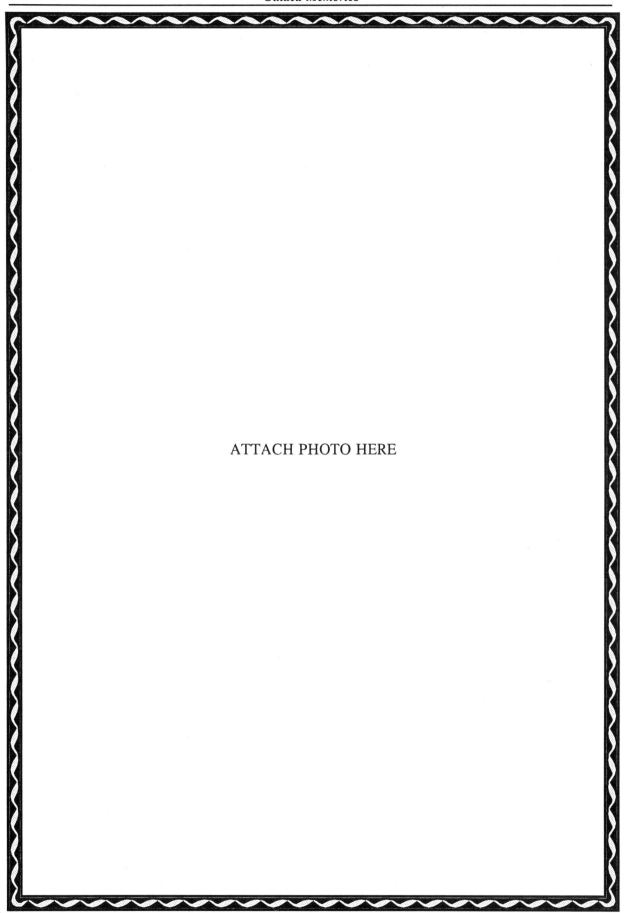

ATTACH PHOTO HERE

WORKSHEET

Who is in this picture and who will I be talking about?

Approximately when was this picture taken?

Notes:

CUE CARDS

(Note: If the person is still living, refer to him or her in the present tense.)

" The name of the person I want to tell you about...."

" The picture was taken in the year......"

" One of the things we shared in common, that made us close was...."

" One of the things that made us different was...."

" What I would like my family (or close friends) to remember about him/her is....."

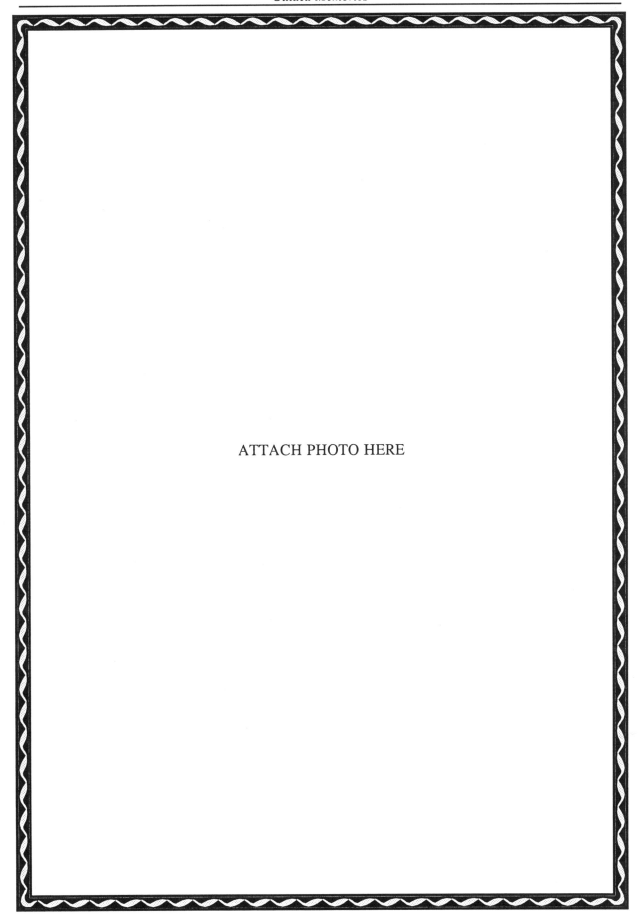

ATTACH PHOTO HERE

 WORKSHEET

Who is in this picture and who will I be talking about?

Approximately when was this picture taken?

Notes:

 CUE CARDS

(Note: If the person is still living, refer to him or her in the present tense.)

" The name of the person I want to tell you about..."

" The picture was taken in the year......"

" One of the things we shared in common, that made us close was...."

" One of the things that made us different was...."

" What I would like my family (or close friends) to remember about him/her is....."

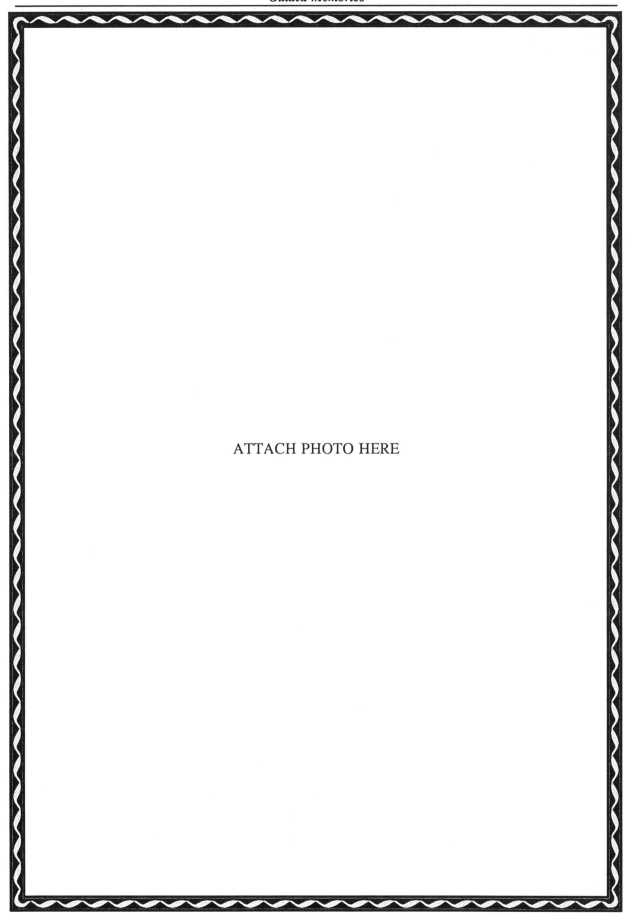

ATTACH PHOTO HERE

There is an appointed time for everything.
And there is a time for every event under heaven
A Time to give birth and a time to die;
A time to plant, and a time to uproot what is planted.
A time to kill, and a time to heal;
A time to tear down, and a time to build up.
A time to weep, and a time to laugh;
A time to mourn, and a time to dance.
A time to throw stones, and a time to gather stones;
A time to embrace, and a time to shun embracing.
A time to search, and a time to give up as lost;
A time to keep, and a time to throw away.
A time to tear apart, and a time to sew together;
A time to be silent, and a time to speak.
A time to love, and a time to hate;
A time for war; and a time for peace.

Ecclesiastes

PART II

Time Flies

Beginning on page 38 you will find six worksheets with six categories of life listed: **(1) Homes, (2) Friends, (3) Romance, (4) Tragedy, (5) Happiness and (6) Travels.** Complete the worksheet for each category and then return to this page and follow the next step, below.

VIDEO STEPS & IDEAS

1. Prepare all video equipment for filming and load with a high quality video cassette.

2. Determine your location for filming and who will operate the camera. It is easiest if someone operates the camera for you, however you can use a tripod and simply walk into the picture while it is recording and begin talking. If you film yourself it is best to use something to sit on, which can be used to focus the camera to ensure that your picture is clear and that your body is centered in the frame. When the filming is completed, walk out of the picture frame and turn the camera off.

3. When ready to film turn on the recorder and use the worksheets and cue cards as your script. Begin with the first category (Homes) and talk freely, referring to the worksheet and cue cards until you have said all you would like to mention. **REMEMBER TO FOLLOW THE NUMBER (#) COLUMN on each worksheet and talk about each memory in chronological order.** When you have finished all six categories label your video with the title *Time Flies* and store in a safe place.

4. **Tips:** • Use page 35 as a **Title Page** by filming it first before you begin recording • Keep the camera rolling with as few breaks as possible • **Don't edit anything!** include the bloopers, laughter, tears, mistakes, shifts of thought, a change of answer etc. Part of the joy for the future viewer is seeing it all.

AUDIO STEPS & IDEAS

1. Prepare your audio equipment for recording. Choose a quiet setting where your voice can be clearly heard and you won't be disturbed by interruptions, phone calls, door bells, etc.

2. Begin with the first category (Homes) and talk freely, referring to the worksheet and cue cards until you have included all you would like to mention. **REMEMBER TO FOLLOW THE NUMBER (#) COLUMN on each worksheet and talk about each memory in chronological order.** When you have finished all six categories label your cassette with the title *Time Flies* and store in a safe place.

3. **Tips:** • Before you begin talking about each category, record what you will be discussing. For example, you might say something like, *" I am going to be talking about the different places I have lived. "* • Keep the recorder running with as few breaks as possible • **<u>Don't edit anything!</u>** include the bloopers, laughter, tears, mistakes, shifts of thought, a change of answer etc. Part of the joy for future listeners is hearing it all.

 **WORKSHEET**

HOMES   Category 1

Under the column below entitled, "Description" write one sentence you can use, when recording, to **describe** all the places you have lived; do not be concerned with order of time. This would include houses, apartments, dorms, military bases, etc. For example, you might write something like, *"The condo on Elm St. by the beach."* When finished, use the number column (#) to place each description in chronological order; 1, 2, 3, 4, etc..

#	DESCRIPTION

CUE CARDS

Use your cue cards freely, paraphrasing, changing the wording or creating your own. Or you can simply read each one out loud and answer accordingly. Don't be afraid to change your answers, or reword what you want to say while recording. You might say something like, *"Let's see..the next home I lived in would be.... what I remember is...uhm...well, let me come back to that, what I want to tell you about right now is...."* Be yourself and forget about editing!!!! If you are currently living in the home you are describing, refer to it in the present tense.

"One of the first homes I can remember living in was in the year...."

"We lived there because...."

(Describe the home) "It was a (big/small) home, with (1,2,3,etc.) bedrooms, the neighborhood was (poor, wealthy, ugly, beautiful, etc.)...."

"One of my favorite memories about the neighborhood is...."

"One of the worst memories about the neighborhood is...."

"The people who lived with me in the house were (Father, Mother, etc.)...."

"I remember that most of the time I lived in this home it was a (happy, sad, etc.) time... because....."

"While we lived in this house I remember the economy (or spirit of the times) being...."

"Some of the things I remember being bought during this time were (T.V. , cars, clothes, pool tables, stereos, toys, furniture, pools, sports equipment, etc.)

"We had a few pets while living in this home, we had a....and...."

"If I could choose any of the homes I listed, to live in forever, it would be....because...."

WORKSHEET

FRIENDS Category 1

Under the column below entitled, "Description" write the names of those friends, from childhood to the present (non-family members) with whom you have shared a close relationship. When finished, use the number column (#) to place each name in chronological order 1, 2, 3, 4, etc., to show when you first met.

#	DESCRIPTION

CUE CARDS

   Use the cue cards freely, paraphrasing, changing the wording or creating your own. Or you can simply read each one and answer accordingly. Don't be afraid to change your answers, or reword what you want to say while recording. You might say something like, *"One of the first friends I met was Bill...uhm...well, now that I think about it I really met Mary first, then Bill, so I think I'll talk about her first, and I can't remember when we first met, but what I do remember is...."* Be yourself and forget about editing!!!! If you are talking about a friend who is still living and you remain in contact with, refer to them in the present tense.

"One of my first friends was...."

(Describe their physical appearance) "She/he looked...."

"We first met...."

"I think the thing we shared most in common, that made us friends was...."

"Some of the things that were different about our personalities were...."

"One of the best times we ever had was when we...."

"One of the worst times we ever had was...."

"If I could go back in time and do anything different in our friendship I would...."

"If I could do anything with this friend again I would...."

"Our relationship changed over time because...."

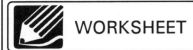 **WORKSHEET**

ROMANCE Category 1

Under the column below entitled, "Description" write the names of those INDIVIDUALS with whom you have shared a romantic relationship (beginning with your youth). When finished, use the number column (#) to place each name in chronological order 1, 2, 3, 4, etc., to show when you first met.

#	DESCRIPTION

CUE CARDS

Use the cue cards freely, paraphrasing, changing the wording or creating your own. Or simply read each one out loud and answer accordingly. Don't be afraid to change your answers, or reword what you want to say while recording. You might say something like, *"One of the things we shared in common was...well...we didn't really have a lot in common, I guess it was more like momentary passion...well, anyway...let me see....what else do I want to talk about?....Oh yeah..one of the best times we ever had was...."* Remember to be yourself and forget about editing!!!! If you are talking about someone you are currently involved with, refer to them in the present tense.

"One of my first romantic relationships was with ...."

(Describe their physical appearance) "She/he looked...."

"We first met...."

"I think the thing we shared most in common was...."

"Some of the things that were different about our personalities were...."

"One of the best times we ever had was when we...."

"One of the worst times we ever had was...."

"If I could go back in time and do anything different in our relationship I would...."

"If I could do anything with this person again I would...."

"Our relationship changed over time because...."

"What I learned from this relationship was...."

 WORKSHEET

TRAGEDY   Category 1

Under the column below entitled, "Description" write one sentence you can use to describe a major tragedy in your life. This may include deaths, accidents, school problems, difficulties, divorce, illness, failures, etc. When finished use the number column (#) to place each description in chronological order 1, 2, 3, 4, etc., to show what time in your life it occurred.

#	DESCRIPTION

CUE CARDS

Use the cue cards freely, paraphrasing, changing the wording or creating your own. Or simply read each one out loud and answer accordingly. Don't be afraid to change your answers, or reword what you want to say while recording. It will probably be difficult to discuss certain issues. Don't be afraid to reveal your emotions! Cry, laugh, pause, etc. Remember to be yourself and forget about editing!!!! If you are talking about a present issue refer to it the present tense.

"The first tragedy (disappointment, etc.) in my life was...."

"The thing that was most difficult about this time in my life was...."

"I think that some of the reasons for this occurring were..."

"The people who were affected by this were (family, friends, etc.)...."

"What I did to deal with this tragedy in my life was...."

"If I could change anything about what happened I would...."

"What I learned from this was...."

 **WORKSHEET**

HAPPINESS Category 1

Under the column below entitled, "Description" write one sentence to describe a time of happiness in your life. This may include marriage, births, education, honors, awards, promotions, achievements, etc.. When finished, use the number column (#) to place each event in chronological order 1, 2, 3, 4, etc., to show what time in your life it occurred.

#	DESCRIPTION

◰ CUE CARDS

Use the cue cards freely, paraphrasing, changing the wording or creating your own. Or simply read each one out loud and answer accordingly. Don't be afraid to change your answers, or reword what you want to say while recording. Remember to be yourself and forget about editing!!!! If you are talking about a present issue refer to it in the present tense.

"One of the first things in my life that brought me a great deal of happiness was...."

"The thing that made this such a great time in my life was...."

"I think that some of the reasons for this happening were..."

"The people who were with me during this time were (family, friends, etc.)...."

"The thing I benefited from the most was...."

"The only thing I might have changed about this is...."

"Of all the accomplishments and happy events in my life, the one I would most like to relive is...."

 WORKSHEET

TRAVELS Category 1

Under the column below entitled, "Description" write one sentence to describe the most enjoyable travels of your life. This may include vacations, business trips, sabbaticals, missions, adventures, explorations, etc. When finished, use the number column (#) to place each description in chronological order 1, 2, 3, 4, etc., to show what time in your life it occurred.

#	DESCRIPTION

CUE CARDS

Use the cue cards freely, paraphrasing, changing the wording or creating your own. Or simply read each one out loud and answer accordingly. Don't be afraid to change your answers, or reword what you want to say while recording. Remember to be yourself and forget about editing!!!! If you are talking about a present issue refer to it the present tense.

"One of the first adventures (travels, etc.) in my life was...."

"The reason I went on this trip was because...."

"I was on this journey for (day, months, years, etc.)..."

"The people who were with me were (family, friends, associates, guides, etc.)...."

"One of the things I didn't enjoy about this was...."

"What I enjoyed most about this journey in my life was...."

"The only thing I might have changed about this was...."

"Of all my travels and adventures in life, the one I would most like to relive is...."

"On this trip we met...."

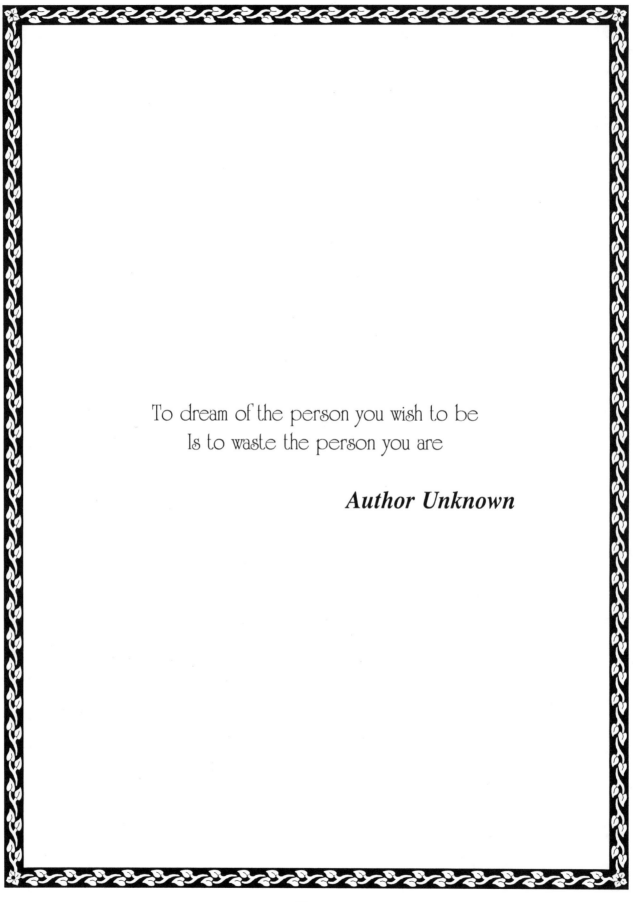

To dream of the person you wish to be
Is to waste the person you are

Author Unknown

PART III

Personality & Opinions

On page 54 begins a series of ninety questions entitled *"Questions Of Preference,"* designed to explore your personality and opinions and how you prefer to relate to the world. This will be a simple process of reading the question and providing an answer. It is not necessary to give an in depth response to each question. However, answer as you wish and, if appropriate, give the reason for your answer. Do not prepare for this exercise by taking notes; rather talk "off the cuff" and be spontaneous, correcting yourself or changing your mind while recording.

 VIDEO STEPS & IDEAS

1. Prepare all video equipment for filming and load with a high quality video cassette.

2. Determine your location for filming and who will operate the camera. It is easiest if someone operates the camera for you, however you can use a tripod and simply walk into the picture while it is recording and begin talking. If you film yourself it is best to use something to sit on, which can be used to focus the camera to ensure that your picture is clear and that your body is centered in the frame. When filming is completed, walk out of the picture frame and turn the camera off.

3. When ready to film turn on the recorder, read each question and give your answer. When you have completed all ninety questions label your video with the title *Personality & Opinions* and store in a safe place.

4. **Tips:** • Use page 51 as a **Title Page** by filming it first before you begin recording • You may want to have someone in the picture with you, asking the questions in interview style • **Don't edit anything!** (try to keep the recorder going) include the bloopers, shots of the sky, laughter, tears, mistakes, shifts of thought, a change of answer etc. Part of the joy for future viewers is seeing it all.

 AUDIO STEPS & IDEAS

1. Prepare your audio equipment for recording. Choose a quiet setting where your voice can be heard clearly and you won't be bothered with interruptions, phone calls, door bells, etc.

2. When ready, turn on the recorder, read each question and give your answer. When you have completed all ninety questions label your cassette with the title, *Personality & Opinions* and store in a safe place.

3. **Tips:** • Before you answer the questions you might record an introduction to what you will be discussing. For example, you might say something like, *" I am going to be reading and answering the questions that deal with my personal opinions and personality"* • If you prefer you could have someone read each question to you, followed by your answer • **Don't edit anything!** include the bloopers, laughter, tears, mistakes, shifts of thought, a change of answer, etc. Part of the joy for the future listeners is hearing it all.

Questions Of Preference

---

1. At a party, am I more likely to be sociable or quiet and to myself?

2. Do I feel a sense of peace most of the time, or do I find myself bored often?

3. What kind of people do I get along better with, people with their feet firmly planted on the ground, or highly imaginative people?

4. Am I more likely to follow my heart or my head?

5. When a new fad or fashion comes to town am I one of the first ones to try it, or could I care less?

6. When I hear a new idea, am I more likely to be skeptical and critical, or anxious to find out more about it?

7. Is it hard or easy to get to know me?

8. Am I more comfortable with giving orders, or following them?

9. Do I think of myself as liberal or conservative?

10. Am I easily swayed by the opinions of others, or am I more likely to be stubborn?

11. When I am embarrassed in front of others, am I able to come back with a witty reply or am I usually at a loss for words?

12. Would I rather have people think of me as determined or warm hearted?

13. Am I the kind of person who makes New Years resolutions and keeps them, or do they fade with time?

---

14. If I were assembling something would I stop and read the directions, or plunge right in?

15. If I needed to solve a personal problem, would I be more likely to seek the opinion of others or believe that no one could give me better advice than myself?

16. Would I rather have people refer to me as someone in touch with their feelings, or someone who is reasonable?

17. Do I think that most of the people who really know me, understand me, or not?

18. Would I rather work for someone who is fun, or someone who I know will get the job done despite his or her attitude?

19. Do I wait for things in life to inspire me, or do I go out looking for it?

21. If I were laid off from work, am I more likely to enjoy the break or start looking for new employment as soon as possible?

22. If I had to read either a book of poems or a newspaper, which would I prefer?

23. Is it better for people to show their feelings or keep them to themselves?

24. Do people consider me opinionated or open minded?

25. Would I rather gamble on something that may lead to bigger possibilities, or stick with a sure thing?

26. Do I have a tendency to take on more than I can handle, or do I know my limits?

27. If I were to tell you, "Let's get together some time," would I call you within the next day or two, or let it slide until you called me?

28. If I thought the truth would hurt someone's feelings would I be more likely to tell a lie or let them know the truth?

29. Am I more likely to do extra work for the money or for the personal satisfaction?

30. If a friend has hurt my feelings am I more likely to confront him or her, or let it slide?

31. When a problem arises am I more likely to blame it on myself or the world around me?

32. Which actors do I identify with the most?

33. What are some of the best books I've ever read?

34. If I could spend one week with anyone who has ever lived, who would it be?

35. If I could relive one day of my life, what day would that be?

36. What are some of my favorite foods?

37. What are my favorite colors?

38. What kind of music do I like and who are my favorite recording artists?

39. Why do people use drugs?

40. What is my favorite kind of pet?

41. What sports do I like most?

42. What do I think happens after death?

43. Where is my favorite place to be alone?

44. How many hours of sleep do I need a night?

45. What's the best way to spend a rainy day?

46. What is the best thing to eat on a hot dog?

47. If I had to choose a world ruler, would it be John Wayne or Gandhi?

48. What religion do I believe in?

49. What is my favorite cologne & perfume?

50. Should there be a death penalty?

51. What's my favorite ice cream?

52. What would I change about my physical appearance if I could?

53. If I could be any super hero, who would I be?

54. If I could make one rule that everyone in the world had to follow, what would it be?

55. If I could have any car, which would I choose?

56. Do I like to shower in the morning or at night?

57. What is the appropriate punishment for murder?

58. Would I rather wear casual clothes or dress clothing?

59. If there were only one magazine to read what should it be?

60. What is the greatest threat to our civilization?

61. What is my favorite holiday?

62. *What is my favorite ride at an amusement park?*

63. *What should the punishment be for child abuse?*

64. *Is alcoholism a disease or a life style?*

65. *What do I think of psychiatrists and psychologists?*

66. *Should people use credit cards?*

67. *Do I think nuclear war is inevitable?*

68. *What is the best drink on a hot day?*

69. *Is it ever O.K. to hit another human being?*

70. *Would I like driving in a car over 100 MPH?*

71. *What is the most enjoyable thing to do after a hard days work?*

72. *What is the best drink on a cold day?*

73. *What is the best climate to live in?*

74. *If I could afford a face lift, would I have one?*

75. *Should street drugs be legalized?*

76. *What is the most expensive gift I have ever received?*

77. *Is there an "unforgivable sin" ?*

78. *What would I like to change about my personality?*

79. *Would I rather eat a bowl of cold cereal, waffles, or eggs and toast for breakfast?*

83. What smells better: an ocean breeze, a fresh cut lawn on a hot summer day, or chocolate chip cookies, just out of the oven?

84. It is O.K. to tell "white lies"?

85. Do I agree with the principle, "An eye for an eye and a tooth for a tooth?"

86. Who is my favorite cartoon character?

87. Is Cinderella just a fairy tale, or is it possible to experience that kind of romantic relationship?

88. Who is the wisest person I have ever met?

89. What are some of my favorite movies?

90. If I could ask God one question, what would it be?

How blessed is the man who finds wisdom,
And the man who gains understanding.
For its profit is better than the profit of silver,
And its gain than fine gold.
She is more precious than jewels;
And nothing you desire compares with her.
Long life is in her right hand;
In her left hand are riches and honor.
Her ways are pleasant ways,
And all her paths are peace.
She is the tree of life to those who take hold of her,
And happy are all who hold her fast.

Proverbs

PART IV

Lessons To Remember

O n pages 64-69 you will find a list of fifty famous quotes from religious and philosophical sources. Read through the list and place a check mark before each quote which you believe reflects the important lessons of life (choose at least fifteen). From among those checked, circle ten. After you have chosen 10 write one quote in each of the ten boxes (beginning on page 70), below the title, *MY TEN LESSONS* and complete the worksheet. If you prefer **you may choose your own lesson!** After finishing the worksheets for all ten lessons, return to this page and follow the instructions for your video or audio recording.

 VIDEO STEPS & IDEAS

1. Prepare all video equipment for filming and load with a high quality video cassette.

2. Determine your location for filming and who will operate the camera. It is easiest if someone operates the camera for you, however you can use a tripod and simply walk into the picture while it is recording and begin talking. If you film yourself it is best to use something to sit on, which can be used to focus the camera to ensure that your picture is clear and that your body is centered in the frame. When filming is completed, walk out of the picture frame and turn the camera off.

3. When ready to film turn on the recorder, read the lesson you will be discussing and, using your worksheet and cue cards, give your answers . When you have completed all ten lessons label your video with the title, *Lessons To Remember* and store in a safe place.

4. **Tips:** • Use page 61 as a **Title Page** by filming it first before you begin recording • You may want to have someone in the picture with you, reading you the questions • **Don't edit anything!** (try to keep the recorder going) include the bloopers, laughter, tears, mistakes, shifts of thought, a change of answer etc. Part of the joy for the future viewer is seeing it all.

 AUDIO STEPS & IDEAS

1. Prepare your audio equipment for recording. Choose a quiet setting where your voice can be heard clearly and you won't be bothered with interruptions, phone calls, door bells, etc.

2. When you are ready, turn on the recorder, read each question out loud and give your answer. When you have completed all Ten Lessons, label your cassette with the title, *Lessons To Remember* and store in a safe place.

3. Tips: • Before you begin talking about each category, record what you will be discussing. For example, you might say something like, *" I am going to be discussing ten lessons of life that I have found to be very important."* • If you prefer you could have someone read each question to you, followed by your answer. • Keep the recorder running with as few breaks as possible • **Don't edit anything!** include the bloopers, laughter, tears, mistakes, shifts of thought, a change of answer, etc. Part of the joy for future listeners is hearing it all.

Lessons Of Life

___ That which has been is that which will be....there is nothing new under the sun.

____ In much wisdom there is much grief, and increasing knowledge results in increasing pain.

___ A poor, yet wise lad is better than an old and foolish king, even though he was born poor in his kingdom.

___ He who loves money will not be satisfied with money.

___ Sorrow is better than laughter, for when a face is sad a heart may be happy.

___ Friendship is only purchased by friendship.

___ It is only the forgiving who are qualified to receive forgiveness.

___ Defeat isn't bitter if you don't swallow it.

___ A man is disturbed not by things, but by the view which he takes of them.

___ Work is the best narcotic.

___ No wise man ever wished to be younger.

___ Anger is a wind that blows out the lamp of the mind.

___ That light that shows us our mistakes is the light that heals us.

___ You talk when you cease to be at peace with your thoughts.

___ Genius is only patience.

___ Whoever has resigned himself to fate, will find that fate accepts his resignation.

___ Be what you wish others to become.

___ To dream of the person you wish to be, is to waste the person you are.

___ Do right and leave the results with God.

___ Never forget that you are part of the people who can be fooled some of the time.

___ Past experience should be a guide post, not a hitching post.

___ Pride goes before a fall.

___ Tact is the unsaid part of what you think.

___ The sleep of those who do right is sweet.

___ Hatred stirs up strife, but love covers all transgressions.

___ Your cup is either half full, or half empty.

___ The righteous man falls seven times, and rises again.

___ Life is difficult.

___ Do not judge lest you be judged.

___ A man who cannot tolerate small ills can never accomplish great things.

___ When the game of life is over the Chess and the Pawn each return to the same box.

___ Lovely flowers fade fast. Weeds last the season.

___ It is of no use to have the book without the learning.

___ A good tree cannot produce bad fruit, nor can a bad tree produce good fruit.

___ No one can serve two masters; for either he will hate the one and love the other, or he will hold to one and despise the other.

___ Better to lose your eye than your good name.

___ To understand your parents love, bear your own children.

___ It is not the sword, but the swordsman.

___ It isn't over until it's over.

_____ It is always necessary to start from a truth in order to teach an error.

_____ To know the road ahead, ask those who are coming back.

_____ A fault denied is twice committed.

_____ Four things cannot be brought back: a word spoken, an arrow discharged, the Divine decree, and past time.

_____ Prove a friend before you seek him.

_____ One cannot lap up the ocean with a shell.

_____ Evil is a hill, everyone gets on his own and speaks about someone else's.

_____ I dreamed a thousand new paths...I woke and walked my old one.

_____ We must learn from life how to suffer it.

___ *God will sell us anything for the price of labor.*

___ *Making the beginning is one third of the work.*

___ *Compete, don't envy.*

___ *We cannot do as we will, we will do as we can.*

Learning is active.
It involves reaching out of the mind.

Dewey

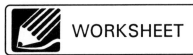 **WORKSHEET**

My Ten Lessons

What this quote means to me in my own words

_____
_____
_____
_____
_____
_____
_____

Why this lesson can be difficult to learn

_____
_____
_____
_____
_____
_____
_____

An example of how I have tried to put this lesson into practice

_____
_____
_____
_____
_____
_____
_____

CUE CARDS

Talking about the lessons of life could require a little more thought than the first three sections of the workbook. However, your worksheet and cue card should provide enough information for you to freely discuss the lesson you have chosen. As with the previous sections of the workbook, do not try to perform the perfect lecture. Talk freely, correcting yourself when necessary without editing.

1. "The lesson I will be discussing is...."

2. "What this quote means to me, in my own words, is...."

3. "One of the reasons this lesson can be difficult to learn is...."

4. (Give an example) "I have tried to put this lesson to practice in my life by...."

 **WORKSHEET**

My Ten Lessons

What this quote means to me in my own words

_____

_____

_____

_____

_____

_____

Why this lesson can be difficult to learn

_____

_____

_____

_____

_____

_____

An example of how I have tried to put this lesson into practice

_____

_____

_____

_____

_____

_____

CUE CARDS

Talking about the lessons of life could require a little more thought than the first three sections of the workbook. However, your worksheet and cue card should provide enough information for you to freely discuss the lesson you have chosen. As with the previous sections of the workbook, do not try to perform the perfect lecture. Talk freely, correcting yourself when necessary without editing.

1. "The lesson I will be discussing is...."

2. "What this quote means to me, in my own words, is...."

3. "One of the reasons this lesson can be difficult to learn is...."

4. (Give an example) "I have tried to put this lesson to practice in my life by...."

 **WORKSHEET**

My Ten Lessons

What this quote means to me in my own words

_____

_____

_____

_____

_____

_____

_____

Why this lesson can be difficult to learn

_____

_____

_____

_____

_____

_____

_____

An example of how I have tried to put this lesson into practice

_____

_____

_____

_____

_____

_____

CUE CARDS

Talking about the lessons of life could require a little more thought than the first three sections of the workbook. However, your worksheet and cue card should provide enough information for you to freely discuss the lesson you have chosen. As with the previous sections of the workbook, do not try to perform the perfect lecture. Talk freely, correcting yourself when necessary without editing.

1. "The lesson I will be discussing is...."

2. "What this quote means to me, in my own words, is...."

3. "One of the reasons this lesson can be difficult to learn is...."

4. (Give an example) "I have tried to put this lesson to practice in my life by...."

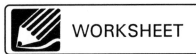 **WORKSHEET**

My Ten Lessons

What this quote means to me in my own words

_____

_____

_____

_____

_____

_____

_____

Why this lesson can be difficult to learn

_____

_____

_____

_____

_____

_____

_____

An example of how I have tried to put this lesson into practice

_____

_____

_____

_____

_____

_____

_____

CUE CARDS

Talking about the lessons of life could require a little more thought than the first three sections of the workbook. However, your worksheet and cue card should provide enough information for you to freely discuss the lesson you have chosen. As with the previous sections of the workbook, do not try to perform the perfect lecture. Talk freely, correcting yourself when necessary without editing.

1. "The lesson I will be discussing is...."

2. "What this quote means to me, in my own words, is...."

3. "One of the reasons this lesson can be difficult to learn is...."

4. (Give an example) "I have tried to put this lesson to practice in my life by...."

 **WORKSHEET**

My Ten Lessons

What this quote means to me in my own words

_____
_____
_____
_____
_____
_____
_____

Why this lesson can be difficult to learn

_____
_____
_____
_____
_____
_____
_____

An example of how I have tried to put this lesson into practice

_____
_____
_____
_____
_____
_____
_____

CUE CARDS

Talking about the lessons of life could require a little more thought than the first three sections of the workbook. However, your worksheet and cue card should provide enough information for you to freely discuss the lesson you have chosen. As with the previous sections of the workbook, do not try to perform the perfect lecture. Talk freely, correcting yourself when necessary without editing.

1. "The lesson I will be discussing is...."

2. "What this quote means to me, in my own words, is...."

3. "One of the reasons this lesson can be difficult to learn is...."

4. (Give an example) "I have tried to put this lesson to practice in my life by...."

WORKSHEET

My Ten Lessons

What this quote means to me in my own words

_____

_____

_____

_____

_____

_____

_____

Why this lesson can be difficult to learn

_____

_____

_____

_____

_____

_____

_____

An example of how I have tried to put this lesson into practice

_____

_____

_____

_____

_____

_____

_____

CUE CARDS

Talking about the lessons of life could require a little more thought than the first three sections of the workbook. However, your worksheet and cue card should provide enough information for you to freely discuss the lesson you have chosen. As with the previous sections of the workbook, do not try to perform the perfect lecture. Talk freely, correcting yourself when necessary without editing.

1. "The lesson I will be discussing is...."

2. "What this quote means to me, in my own words, is...."

3. "One of the reasons this lesson can be difficult to learn is...."

4. (Give an example) "I have tried to put this lesson to practice in my life by...."

 WORKSHEET

My Ten Lessons

What this quote means to me in my own words

_____

_____

_____

_____

_____

_____

_____

Why this lesson can be difficult to learn

_____

_____

_____

_____

_____

_____

An example of how I have tried to put this lesson into practice

_____

_____

_____

_____

_____

_____

CUE CARDS

Talking about the lessons of life could require a little more thought than the first three sections of the workbook. However, your worksheet and cue card should provide enough information for you to freely discuss the lesson you have chosen. As with the previous sections of the workbook, do not try to perform the perfect lecture. Talk freely, correcting yourself when necessary without editing.

1. "The lesson I will be discussing is...."

2. "What this quote means to me, in my own words, is...."

3. "One of the reasons this lesson can be difficult to learn is...."

4. (Give an example) "I have tried to put this lesson to practice in my life by...."

 **WORKSHEET**

My Ten Lessons

What this quote means to me in my own words

_____

_____

_____

_____

_____

_____

_____

Why this lesson can be difficult to learn

_____

_____

_____

_____

_____

_____

An example of how I have tried to put this lesson into practice

_____

_____

_____

_____

_____

_____

▱ CUE CARDS

Talking about the lessons of life could require a little more thought than the first three sections of the workbook. However, your worksheet and cue card should provide enough information for you to freely discuss the lesson you have chosen. As with the previous sections of the workbook, do not try to perform the perfect lecture. Talk freely, correcting yourself when necessary without editing.

1. "The lesson I will be discussing is...."

2. "What this quote means to me, in my own words, is...."

3. "One of the reasons this lesson can be difficult to learn is...."

4. (Give an example) "I have tried to put this lesson to practice in my life by...."

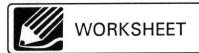

WORKSHEET

My Ten Lessons

What this quote means to me in my own words

_____

_____

_____

_____

_____

_____

_____

Why this lesson can be difficult to learn

_____

_____

_____

_____

_____

_____

An example of how I have tried to put this lesson into practice

_____

_____

_____

_____

_____

_____

_____

CUE CARDS

Talking about the lessons of life could require a little more thought than the first three sections of the workbook. However, your worksheet and cue card should provide enough information for you to freely discuss the lesson you have chosen. As with the previous sections of the workbook, do not try to perform the perfect lecture. Talk freely, correcting yourself when necessary without editing.

1. "The lesson I will be discussing is...."

2. "What this quote means to me, in my own words, is...."

3. "One of the reasons this lesson can be difficult to learn is...."

4. (Give an example) "I have tried to put this lesson to practice in my life by...."

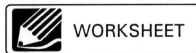 **WORKSHEET**

My Ten Lessons

What this quote means to me in my own words

_____

_____

_____

_____

_____

_____

_____

Why this lesson can be difficult to learn

_____

_____

_____

_____

_____

_____

_____

An example of how I have tried to put this lesson into practice

_____

_____

_____

_____

_____

_____

_____

CUE CARDS

Talking about the lessons of life could require a little more thought than the first three sections of the workbook. However, your worksheet and cue card should provide enough information for you to freely discuss the lesson you have chosen. As with the previous sections of the workbook, do not try to perform the perfect lecture. Talk freely, correcting yourself when necessary without editing.

1. "The lesson I will be discussing is...."

2. "What this quote means to me, in my own words, is...."

3. "One of the reasons this lesson can be difficult to learn is.."

4. (Give an example) "I have tried to put this lesson to practice in my life by...."

CONGRATULATIONS!

You have now completed your Guided Memories Personal Autobiography on Audio Or Video Cassette. To protect your recordings order a video or audio cassette album by sending in the order form on the following page. Store your album in a safe place for future generations to enjoy.

TO ORDER ADDITIONAL COPIES OF THE GUIDED MEMORIES WORKBOOK, FILL OUT THE ORDER FORM BELOW:

Name: (Please Print)_____

Address:_____

City/State/Zip _____

Total Number Of Books Ordered: _____

Times ($11.95 each) Sub Total: _____

Sales Tax (CA only. 99¢) _____

Shipping & Handling ($ 2. 00) _____

Total Due: _____

Paid By : Check___Mastercard ___ Visa___

Signature_____

Credit Card #:_____ Exp. ____

MAIL ORDERS TO:
R&Z PUBLISHING
245-M Mt. Hermon Rd. #280
Scotts Valley, CA 95066

For a Professional Video Production of your Guided Memories Call: (408) 438-3327

Guided Memories Albums

Available for Video or Audio Cassette. Preserve your recorded memories in an attractive video or audio cassette album. Album holds 6 audio cassettes or 2 Video tapes.

$12.95 Each!

Choose From Two Different Albums

Inside Cassette Album

Holds 6 Cassettes Code # AO6

Inside Video Album

Holds 2 Videos Code # VO2

ORDER FORM Make Checks Payable To: *R&Z Publishing*

Code#	Description	Qty.	Total
____	_____	___	___
____	_____	___	___

Total Number of Albums Ordered _____

Total Cost ($12.95) _____

Sales Tax (CA Residents Only, $1.07) _____

Shipping & Handling ($2.00) _____

TOTAL DUE: _____

MAIL ORDERS TO:
R&Z Publishing
245-M Mt. Hermon Rd #280
Scotts Valley, CA 95066

Name: (Please Print)_____

Address_____

City/State/Zip_____

Paid By : Check____ Mastercard ____ Visa ____ Exp. Date_____

Credit Card #:_____ Signature_____

ABOUT THE AUTHOR

David Zuccolotto is a marriage and family therapist living on the Monterey Bay of California with his wife Kelly and their three children, David, Michael and Daniella. Mr. Zuccolotto's work as a clinician, consultant and lecturer has spanned a period of fifteen years, reaching churches, psychiatric hospitals, private practices, government agencies, businesses and colleges. He is also the creator and author of the syndicated comic strip, *Dr. Sickmund Fred.* His other works include *The Truth About Psychology*, Synergetic Publications; and *The Laughagraph: Building Self-Esteem Through Humor*, R & Z Publishing Company.